The Obstinate Pen

Frank W. Dormer

Henry Holt and Company
NEW YORK

Uncle Flood unwrapped his
new pen and laid it on the desk.
It promptly stood at attention.

Uncle Flood shivered
with delight.

"I MUST HAVE SILENCE WHEN I WRITE!"

Flood yelled at his nephew.

Horace left.

Uncle Flood removed the cap
from his pen and began to write:
The following story is all true.
But the pen did not write that sentence.
What the pen wrote was this:

You have a BIG noSe.

Uncle Flood could only stare at the paper.
He wrote again: *The following story is all true.*
The pen wrote:

You have Eyes as large as dinner plates.

Flood's mouth dropped open.

"**PEN!**" he yelled.

"You'd better write what I want this time or I will throw you out the window!"

The following story is all true, he wrote.
   The pen wrote:
Your hair is like a BIRD'S NEST.

The pen flew out the window
and landed in Officer Wonkle's ear.

"EEK!"
said Officer Wonkle.

"Is something wrong?" asked a woman.

"A pen," Officer Wonkle said.
"Just what I needed."

He began to write a ticket to the woman.
NAME: *Miss Glenda Weeble.*

But the pen did not write
that sentence.

What the pen wrote
was this:

NAME: Kiss that girl!!

INFRACTION: _____

_____

LOCATION: _____

_____

REPORTING OFFICER: _____

Officer Wonkle's face turned red.
He started another ticket.
NAME: *Miss Glenda Weeble*.
The pen wrote:

"Are you all right?" asked Miss Weeble.
She thought the officer was very handsome.
"Sorry, ma'am. It's this pen." He scratched
out the last line and tried again.

NAME: *Miss Glenda Weeble.*
The pen wrote:

Officer Wonkle made up his mind.
He threw the pen away and pressed
a kiss on Miss Weeble's cheek.

The pen landed in the street. It stuck to
the wheel of Mrs. Norkham Pigeon-Smythe's
automobile. The pen made an awful *tick-tick*
sound until Mrs. Pigeon-Smythe's driver,
Druthers, stopped and pulled it out.

"Izza pen," said Druthers.
He handed it to Mrs. Norkham
Pigeon-Smythe.

"Oh, what a sturdy little pen,"
she said. "Druthers, fetch me a
bit of stationery. I must use this
pen to write my memoir."

Soon Mrs. Pigeon-Smythe sat down to write her memoir. She wrote: "I, Mrs. Norkham Pigeon-Smythe, related to the Great King of Farflungdom, have lived a very lush life."

The pen wrote:

Mrs. Pigeon-Smythe burst out laughing. "Oh dear, what a precocious pen! I must tell everyone about it."

She began writing again,
and the pen wrote:

She laughed even louder.

Mrs. Norkham
Pigeon-Smythe
ordered a Large
Dinner Party and
invited every one
of her friends to
try the pen.

It insulted a duke,
three duchesses,
and the maid.

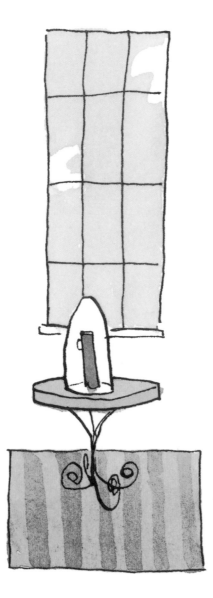

After the Large Dinner Party,
Mrs. Pigeon-Smythe placed the
pen under glass in a room in her
house that no one visited.

So the pen did what any prisoner would do.

It broke out.

It landed on the ground
and stood straight up . . .

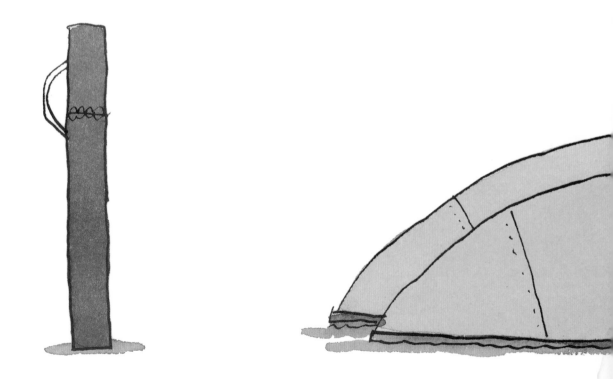

. . . where it was picked up by Horace.

He looked at its
shiny, smooth barrel.

He admired its
pointed, flexy tip.

Horace walked to the park. He sat down.
He pulled out a sheet of paper . . .

. . . and began to draw.

And the pen . . .

. . . let him.

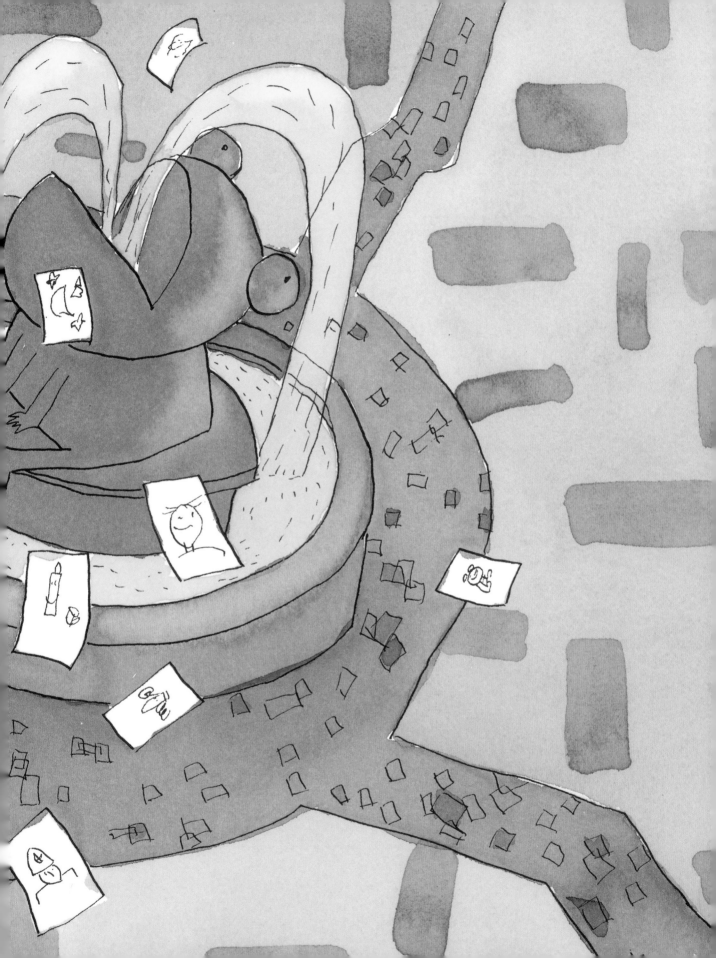

To the one and only Seuss—
You know who you are.

Henry Holt and Company, LLC
Publishers since 1866
175 Fifth Avenue
New York, New York 10010
mackids.com

Henry Holt® is a registered trademark of Henry Holt and Company, LLC.
Copyright © 2012 by Frank W. Dormer
All rights reserved.

Library of Congress Cataloging-in-Publication Data
Dormer, Frank W.
The obstinate pen / Frank W. Dormer. — 1st ed.
p.   cm.
Summary: Uncle Flood is very pleased with his new pen until he tries to write
with it and finds that it writes only what it wants to for him, and the series of people
who try it after him, until finally his nephew Horace tries something new.
ISBN 978-0-8050-9295-0
[1. Pens—Fiction. 2. Writing—Fiction. 3. Obstinacy—Fiction.] I. Title.
PZ7.D7283Obs 2011   [E]—dc22   2010031794

First Edition—2012 / Designed by April Ward
Printed in China by Toppan Leefung Printing Ltd.,
Dongguan City, Guangdong Province
1 3 5 7 9 10 8 6 4 2